Addie's Forever Friend

Laurie Lawlor

illustrated by Helen Cogancherry

ALBERT WHITMAN & COMPANY
MORTON GROVE, ILLINOIS

Library of Congress Cataloging-in-Publication Data

Lawlor, Laurie
Addie's forever friend / written by Laurie Lawlor; illustrated by Helen Cogancherry.
p. cm.

Prequel to: Addie across the prairie.
Summary: While her father is looking for a homestead in the Dakotas, Addie and her
mother and brothers spend the summer with her aunt and uncle in Sabula, Iowa,
where Addie and her best friend have an exciting adventure on the Fourth of July.

ISBN 0-8075-0164-6
[1. Brothers and sisters—Fiction. 2. Family life—Iowa—Fiction.
3. Friendship—Fiction. 4. Iowa—Fiction.] I. Cogancherry, Helen, ill. II. Title.
PZ7.L4189Ad 1997
[Fic]—dc21
96-54016
CIP
AC

Designed by Scott Piehl.

Also by Laurie Lawlor
Daniel Boone
How to Survive Third Grade
The Real Johnny Appleseed
Second-Grade Dog

Other books about Addie and her family
Addie Across the Prairie
Addie's Dakota Winter
Addie's Long Summer
George on His Own

For Ruby

Contents

Chapter One

Too Afraid

"Watch me, Addie Mills!" eight-year-old Eleanor shouted. She balanced atop the broad back of her patient horse, Vulcan, who stood belly-deep in the Mississippi River. With a loud whoop, she leapt into the water, arms flying. *Splash!*

"Good jump!" Addie cheered from shore. That Eleanor Fitzgerald!

"Your turn," Eleanor called.

Addie shook her head. "Too cold."

"Too afraid's more like it," seven-year-old George shouted from the river. He quickly climbed on top of Vulcan, closed his eyes, and toppled backward, stiff as a fence post. *Ker-splash!*

Addie pretended she hadn't heard George's nasty comment. But her cheeks burned as she smacked and kneaded another sand cake.

Secretly, Addie wished she could swim. Now that she was nearly nine years old, there seemed no excuse for not knowing how. But the one time Pa had tried to teach her, she had given up right away. How choked and blind and scared she had felt! The river was too cold, too dark, too full of secret currents and hidden fish.

"Lew, come away from the water," Addie called

to her three-year-old brother. "Try one of my special Fourth-of-July cakes. One bite and you'll set off a secret firecracker."

Lew pouted and dug his toe in the sand.

"You can't go in the river," Addie explained. "You're too little."

Angrily, Lew plunked himself down in the wet sand and began burying his shoes. Addie sighed. At least she didn't have to watch Burton Grant today, too. For once, her youngest brother, who was nearly two, had stayed home with Mother. But why, oh why, on this perfect day in July, did she have to take care of pesky Lew while George got to spend the whole time with Eleanor? It wasn't fair. Eleanor was Addie's best friend, not George's.

"Bet you can't splash like an exploding cannon-ball," George bragged. He stood on the horse and hurled himself into the water, holding both skinny knees close to his chest. *Splash!*

"That's nothing," Eleanor jeered. "You should see what the big boys from town do at night. When no one's looking, they do double flips off the back of steamboats and land in the water with a terrific smack. Someday I'm going to try that."

"You can't," George replied.

"Why not?" Eleanor demanded.

"Girls aren't strong enough to do double flips."

"Are too."

"Aren't."

"Are too."

Eleanor shoved George underwater. He came up in a fury of spray.

"Come in now!" Addie called when the water fight began to look serious. "Your lips are turning blue. Besides, it's time to eat."

Dripping, Eleanor staggered to shore pulling Vulcan. She tied the gentle giant to a tree. "Hurrah! Cake for lunch!"

George licked his lips and rushed out of the water. "Cake? Where?"

Eleanor bent double with laughter. She pointed to Addie's cakes. "Fresh Mississippi mud cakes, George!"

George scowled.

"Aunt Ida made beautiful ham sandwiches," Addie said. She lifted the linen napkin that covered the picnic basket. Back on the farm, Mother prepared simple bread and butter for their picnics. But since Addie, her brothers, and Mother were living with Aunt Ida and Uncle Manfred in their big house in Sabula, Iowa, they had fancy meat sandwiches wrapped in newspaper and a Mason jar of cool, fresh lemonade.

"Don't tear the newspaper," Eleanor said with her mouth full. "Addie can read to us later, can't you, Addie?"

Addie nodded. She was proud that she was the

only one among them who could make out the big words in the *Sabula Gazette*.

"Give me a swig!" George said, wiping the crumbs from his face with his grubby hand. He took the jar of lemonade and tipped it back.

"You don't have to be so greedy," Addie said.

Eleanor rolled her eyes in agreement.

George made a rude face. For the next several moments, no one said anything. They were too busy eating. The sleepy river glinted with sunlight. Frogs croaked. Birds darted overhead. This bend of the Mississippi was far enough from town that the children couldn't smell awful odors from the Sabula Packing Company. They couldn't hear the Chicago, Clinton, Dubuque, and Minneapolis Railroad cars squealing over the iron bridge. It was quiet and peaceful.

"I wanna go home," Lew said as soon as he'd finished eating.

"What home?" George said slyly.

"Home!" Lew whined.

"We can't go to our farm till Pa gets back from out West," George said. "Until then, we have to stay at Aunt Ida's. We don't have a real home anymore."

Lew began to whimper.

"Don't be so mean, George. He doesn't understand," Addie hissed. She turned to Lew and explained, "We're just staying with Aunt Ida for a little while longer, Lew. Don't worry."

"Grandpa! Want Grandpa!" Lew insisted.

"We can't go to Grandpa's. Grandpa's gone. He went on a trip to see his sister," George said. "We're stuck at Aunt Ida's."

Lew pouted.

"Ignore your horrid brother, Skeeter," Eleanor said. She handed Lew what was left of her sandwich. "I think that's a good nickname for Lew, don't you, Addie? He's just about as big as a mosquito."

Addie smiled. Eleanor was so clever sometimes. Lew stuffed the rest of the sandwich into his mouth. He ambled a short way along the river's edge. He stopped, sat down, and poked sticks into the sand.

"Don't wander too far, Skeeter," Eleanor called after him. "Now read to us, will you, Addie?"

"None of that mushy lovey-dovey poetry stuff. I hate it," George said. He handed Addie the newspaper sheets. Then he stretched out in the sand, his cap over his eyes. "Read about the Sabula Brass-and-Cornet Concert Band that's going to march in the Fourth-of-July parade." He pursed his lips together and made a tooting sound. "Only two days till the big day. I'm going to eat till I puke."

Addie and Eleanor exchanged looks of disgust. "Let's see," Addie said, examining the newspaper. "There's nothing about the band. What about 'The Cowboy's Real Life'?"

"Perfect!" George exclaimed.

"'The cowboy's life is an exciting one, hardy and adventurous—'"

"That's the life for me," George announced. "Hardy and adventurous."

"Be quiet, George, and let her read," Eleanor complained.

"'He eats in a tent, lives on a steed, sleeps under the stars, seldom with a blanket or fire—'"

"What's a steed?" George interrupted.

Addie rubbed her chin. "I think it's a horse."

"But not a horse as old and slow as Vulcan," George added. "A horse that's young and fast, right?"

"Will you stop interrupting?" Eleanor said. "Vulcan is a very good horse. He's not afraid of anything."

"'The cowboy is an expert with the lariat,'" Addie continued, "'fearless of horse or herd.'" As soon as she finished reading about how the cowboy must be quick to catch cows with his lariat, George jumped up. He began throwing Vulcan's looped rope around a stump.

"Good," Addie said when George was out of earshot. "Now we can finally talk."

CHAPTER TWO

Secrets

"YOU LOOK LIKE YOU'VE GOT A SECRET," Eleanor whispered. "What is it?"

Addie smiled.

"Is it about your father? I heard he's looking for land in Dakota. When's he coming back?"

Addie's grin disappeared. She missed her father. It seemed as if he'd been gone forever. "Mother says he'll be back by August. In time for threshing."

"My uncle went to Dakota to look for gold. He told me it's mostly Indian warriors and snakes and blizzards. Why's your pa thinking of moving you there?"

"He's *not*," Addie said. "He's just helping our neighbors, Ed and Will, look for land. They're the ones who want to homestead."

"If I were your father," Eleanor continued, "I wouldn't waste my time looking for some dried-up patch of ground. I'd dig for gold and get rich quick."

Addie bit her lip.

"And all the time you're staying with your aunt and uncle, did you ever wonder what's happening back at your farmhouse?" Eleanor continued with enthusiasm. "What if some runaway horse thieves have moved in and made your place their hideout?"

Addie turned away from Eleanor. She rolled up the newspapers and stuffed them inside the picnic basket. Moving to Dakota? Digging for gold? Hidden outlaws? Eleanor's imagination was running wild again. Still, her words worried Addie.

What if Pa hadn't told her the whole truth? After the big flood had washed away their harvest, he'd seemed so anxious each time the rent was due. For the past two winters, supper had often been nothing more than boiled porridge with a little milk. Late at night, she'd seen him plotting new plans with pencil and paper at the kitchen table. What if he'd already come up with some new scheme to take her family far away to an empty wilderness? She shivered.

"Addie," Eleanor said, giving her a start, "you still haven't shared your secret."

Addie crossed her arms and held her elbows tight. She wouldn't worry about moving. Not now. Not when she had such a wonderful secret.

"I'm your best friend," Eleanor said. "You have to tell me."

Addie looked over her shoulder to make sure her brothers weren't listening. George was still practicing with the pretend lariat, and Lew was busy digging a hole. She took a deep breath. "I might be getting a baby sister."

Eleanor made a clucking noise with her tongue. "That's all? I'd gladly give you one of my three sisters to keep for good."

Addie was disappointed. Why wasn't Eleanor thrilled with her news?

"And what if you don't get a girl?" Eleanor said. "Another boy will make *four* brothers! If that happens, you'd better run away. That's what I'd do."

Addie's shoulders sank. She had never thought that the baby might be a boy. For days she'd only thought how wonderful it would be to have a sister.

Someone to help her with washing dishes and peeling potatoes. Someone to share stories and secrets. Someone who wouldn't behead her dolls or ambush her tea parties. "Mother said she thinks it's going to be a girl," Addie said in a small voice. "I heard her tell Aunt Ida."

"Sometimes mothers are wrong," Eleanor said wisely. "Ma was all set to call Abigail 'William' before she was born. She'd even made her a boy's blue bonnet. Well, we'll just have to hope for the best." She stood up, stretched, and yawned. "Speaking of brothers, what happened to Skeeter?"

Addie jumped to her feet. She could see George galloping on a pretend horse among the trees. But where was her younger brother? The riverbank was empty. "Lew!" she shouted, her heart beating fast.

Addie and Eleanor dashed around the bend in the river just in time to hear a splash and a cry. Lew's chubby arm rose above the dark water. More splashes. Addie stopped, frozen. "Lew!" she screamed. She had to save him, but how could she? Her legs refused to budge.

"Get him before he's caught in the current!" George's voice boomed. He rushed past Addie and dove into the river.

"Where is he?" Eleanor shouted. She quickly waded in after George.

"I've got him!" George called. He tugged something pale and limp. He fell and stood again. "Help me!"

Eleanor made a grab. Together they managed to hold Lew's head above water and haul him to shore.

Addie watched, trembling.

"Turn him upside down!" Eleanor ordered.

George did as he was told.

Water rushed from Lew's mouth. He coughed. "Let me up!" he hollered.

"Skeeter, are you all right?" Eleanor asked,

crouching beside the little boy. Addie crept closer.

"He looks fine to me," George said. He wiped sand from his brother's forehead with the tail of his soggy shirt. His hair stood straight up.

"Where's my stick?" Lew demanded.

"Way downriver by now. We'll get you another," Eleanor said. She picked him up and offered him to Addie.

Addie held Lew close and blinked back hot tears. She felt so ashamed. Lew had nearly drowned, and she'd been too afraid to go into the river to save him.

"I'll get Vulcan," George volunteered. "We better go home now." He sounded so grown-up and helpful, not a bit like himself. This only made Addie feel worse. She was the oldest. She was supposed to be the responsible one.

"Put me down," Lew whined. "You're squeezing too hard."

"Don't ever run off like that again, Lew," Addie

said. She set him down and wiped her eyes. Then she turned to Eleanor and asked softly, "Can you teach me to swim? I mean, if you promise not to tell George?"

"I'll teach you if you really want to learn." Eleanor paused to pick up the picnic basket. "To make it a fair trade, you can help me. I have something special planned. Will you give me a hand?"

Addie nodded hesitantly. "What kind of help?"

"A Fourth-of-July surprise," Eleanor said in a mysterious voice. "I still have to work out the details."

"Is this another of your magnificent, new, wonderful ideas?"

Eleanor nodded proudly. Then she beamed down at Lew. "Come on, Skeeter, I'll race you back to town."

CHAPTER THREE

Aunt Ida's Praying Chair

BY THE TIME ADDIE and her brothers returned to Aunt Ida's, Lew seemed to have forgotten his accident. He shouted at George and ran around the pump. "Don't come inside till you wash up," Addie commanded. As usual, her brothers paid no attention to her.

Addie opened the back door. Outside, heavy green shutters framed all the windows of her aunt's big white house. Inside, fancy lace curtains and roll-down shades kept out the bright sun. The cool, shady rooms smelled pleasantly of roses and lemon-oil furniture polish.

Addie tiptoed across the spotless kitchen floor and set the picnic basket on the table. "Aunt Ida?" she called, hoping to find her aunt alone.

No answer.

"Aunt Ida?" she called again.

"Come in, child," Aunt Ida said. "I'm in the parlor."

Even though they had been living with Aunt Ida and Uncle Manfred for nearly a month, Addie still wasn't used to the thick carpeting that seemed to spring up under her feet as she walked into the parlor. It was the fanciest room in their fancy house. Addie and her brothers had been forbidden by

Mother ever to enter unless Aunt Ida invited them. "Too many breakable treasures," Mother had warned.

Aunt Ida sat in a creaking wicker rocker with a frilly skirt around the bottom. Addie secretly called it Aunt Ida's praying chair because this was the place her aunt always sat when she read the Bible. "How was your picnic?" Aunt Ida asked, smiling.

"Delicious," Addie replied. She decided she'd mention Lew's accident another time. Right now she had other questions that needed answering.

"Your mother's sleeping. Poor thing needs some rest. Burt's napping, too," Aunt Ida said. "We won't bother them now, will we?" She closed the Bible in her lap.

Addie took a deep breath. "Aunt Ida, you've read a lot of books. All the relatives and neighbors come to you for advice. That's why I want to ask you something."

Aunt Ida looked flustered. "Can your question wait until your mother wakes up? She's probably better at this kind of thing than I am."

Addie shook her head. "No, I want to ask *you*."

"Well," Aunt Ida said nervously, "I suppose I should be flattered you think I'm so wise."

Addie looked over her shoulder. Any minute she expected her brothers to burst through the door and ruin everything. "Aunt Ida, how did you learn to swim?"

"Oh, child!" Aunt Ida laughed her wonderful deep laugh. "I never learned to swim. Swimming is dangerous. It's not something a proper lady does."

Addie frowned. She thought of how much fun George and Eleanor had jumping from Vulcan into the river. Then she thought of Lew flapping help-lessly in the water. Learning to swim was something she *had* to do, whether it was ladylike or not.

"I don't mean to poke fun at your question," Aunt

Ida said, "but I don't know the first thing about swimming. You look so fretful. Is there something else on your mind?"

Addie twisted her apron sash. "Do you know when Pa's coming back?"

The praying chair creaked. "Soon, child," Aunt Ida said, and stood up. She placed the Bible on the bookshelf. "Do you miss him?"

Addie nodded. "Would you miss us if we moved away?"

"But you're not going anywhere," Aunt Ida insisted. "You and your family are staying right here in Sabula where you belong."

"I mean, would you miss us if we *did* move away?"

Aunt Ida put her arm around Addie. "Of course, child. I'd miss you and your brothers and your father, and I'd surely miss your mother. Ever since we were young, your mother has been the closest of all my sisters."

Addie puzzled over this. She had never considered that her silver-haired aunt might have once been young.

"You know, Addie," Aunt Ida continued, "sisters are forever friends."

Forever friends. Addie liked the sound of that.

Sometimes Addie played with her cousins, but Eleanor was her best friend. Still, even she and Eleanor had arguments. Once, Eleanor had refused to speak to her for two whole days because Addie said her hair needed combing. No, a sister would never act like that. A sister was a sister for life— messy hair or not. Addie tugged on Aunt Ida's sleeve. "When exactly will the new baby get here?"

Aunt Ida blushed. "Soon enough. Babies come when they're ready."

Addie felt more confused than ever. *Soon enough?* Did that mean tomorrow? Or next week? How many days would she have to wait? She couldn't remember very much about when Lew was born. She tried to recall how long it had taken for Burt to be born. When Dr. Ayers had come to the house, she and George had been sent away to pick wild strawberries. When they returned, there was Burt, purple-faced, ugly, and howling like a coyote pup. She felt certain a baby sister would be much prettier.

"Aunt Ida," Addie asked, "is there some way to make sure this baby is a girl?"

"Only God can decide that," Aunt Ida replied.

Addie gripped the back of the rocker. She thought and thought. There had to be something she could do to make sure she got a sister instead of another brother. Then she had an idea.

"Now go and call your brothers while I make sure supper's ready on time," Aunt Ida said. "Your Uncle Manfred is very particular about eating on schedule these days. He has so much to get done before the Fourth of July." She bustled to the kitchen.

Addie waited until Aunt Ida was gone. Then she quickly sat in the praying chair. Slowly, she rocked the creaking chair back and forth while she prayed over and over for a forever friend—a beautiful baby sister. Then, just for good measure, she prayed for Pa's speedy return. And last of all, she prayed that she'd finally learn to swim. "Please, God," she whispered, "by the Fourth of July and thank you very much, amen."

That evening after supper, Addie watched her mother as she struggled to push her chair back, stand up, and clear plates from the table. Mother sang softly as she worked. This meant she was happy. Addie took this as a good sign and felt pleased.

"Becca, sit down. We have a hired girl coming in later to do that work," Aunt Ida insisted.

"Oh, I don't mind," Mother said. Then she kissed her ladylike sister on the top of her head, much to Aunt Ida's surprise, and disappeared into the kitchen.

Lew tap-tap-tapped his spoon against the table. Uncle Manfred folded his napkin and looked sternly at him over the top of his glasses. "I'm afraid I already have one telegraph operator at the train station. I do not need another, Lew."

Lew stopped tapping. His lip quivered.

"Don't cry, Skeeter," George said, grinning. "Can't you tell Uncle Manfred's just joking?"

"Skeeter. What kind of name is that?" Mother said, returning to the table. She stroked Lew's face, and he smiled up at her.

"Skeeter means 'little mosquito.' Eleanor made it up," George said. "I told her she couldn't do a double flip off the back of a steamboat because she was a girl, and she nearly drowned me. Then Lew fell in the river, and he would have drowned for sure except I saved him. How do you like that?"

Addie kicked George under the table, but it was too late.

"Gracious!" Aunt Ida exclaimed.

Mother's face filled with alarm. "Perhaps you children shouldn't go down to the river anymore."

"It's very dangerous," Aunt Ida agreed. "You know what happened three years ago. That poor, poor child—"

Uncle Manfred drummed the table with his fingers. "Please don't tell that story again, dear. We've all heard it a thousand times."

Aunt Ida dabbed her eyes with a dainty handkerchief. "I remember as if it were only yesterday. That little girl fell in during the big flood and was swept away and never found."

"And Addie can't even swim," Mother said in a hushed voice.

Addie stared down at her clenched hands in her lap. She felt so small and stupid and helpless.

"Well, I can swim," George boasted. "Don't worry, Mother."

Addie kicked him again, harder.

"The current's the danger," Aunt Ida said. "I'm glad you reached your brother in time, George."

George beamed.

Addie frowned. What a show-off! She wanted to kick George a third time.

"You children cannot underestimate the power of the Mississippi. From now on, I insist that you take proper precautions. Only swimmers are allowed in the water. That includes you, Lew," Uncle Manfred said.

Lew looked very unhappy.

Uncle Manfred cleared his throat. "Now, we've had enough dire warnings for one evening. I have other news that I think will interest you."

"Is it about the Sabula Brass-and-Cornet Concert Band in the Fourth-of-July parade?" George asked eagerly.

Uncle Manfred grinned. "No. It's about a trip I'm

making to your farm to be sure all is well. I'm going bright and early tomorrow morning. And this time I'm going to take one of you along."

"Me!" George begged.

"May I?" Addie asked politely. "Please, sir?"

"To be perfectly fair, we will draw straws to see who goes. The longer straw wins."

Uncle Manfred loved games of chance. He went into the kitchen and came back with two straws from a broom. He held the straws so they looked exactly the same length as they poked out of the top of his fist.

George grabbed a straw. "Try and beat that!"

Uncle Manfred walked around to the other side of the table.

Addie took the remaining straw from his hand. She smiled. Hers was longer. Then, "Ouch!" she cried, and rubbed her leg where George had kicked her.

"What's wrong?" Mother asked.

"Nothing," Addie said. She gave George a nasty look.

"On your trip tomorrow," Mother said, "I'd like you to bring back some of the baby clothes from the chest of drawers in the hallway."

"Baby clothes?" George howled. "Those will be a tight squeeze for you, Burt." He gave his little brother's fat stomach a pat.

"George, the clothes aren't for Burt," Mother said. "They're for the new baby."

George's jaw dropped.

Now it was Addie's turn to gloat. She'd known about the new baby for a week!

"Wouldn't it be nice if Addie got a sister?" Aunt Ida said, smiling at Addie.

Addie grinned. She was going to choose clothes for the baby. It was an important job.

"Sisters!" George said, and groaned. "Who wants

another sister? Always bossing and complaining. If the baby's a girl, I'll float it down the river on a chunk of wood."

Uncle Manfred chuckled. "I'm sure you'll love the baby, George, no matter what it is."

CHAPTER FOUR

Homesick

"Time's a wastin'," Uncle Manfred said the next morning. He helped Addie into the buggy.

She hoped she looked very grown-up. The quiet streets of Sabula sloped lazily toward the river. A few fishermen cast their lines along the waterfront. A steamboat whistle blew. From the Illinois side of the Mississippi came the familiar, lonely cry of the early morning train about to cross the big bridge.

Addie sat up straight and proud beside her famous uncle, the head stationmaster in town. They headed down Pearl Street, past the store clerks sweeping boardwalks and unrolling store awnings. Uncle Manfred exchanged hellos with a man standing on the porch of the Eldridge House, the biggest hotel in Sabula.

When the buggy reached the Sabula Packing Company, the smell of hog was so strong it nearly took Addie's breath away. She held her nose and watched a hog driver with a long pole guide a herd of noisy hogs along a wooden chute. The raggedy man called out in a loud sing-song voice:

Hog up! Hog up!
Forty cents a day and no dinner,
straw bed and no cover,
corn bread and no butter.
Hog up! Hog up!

"Why is he singing to the hogs?" Addie asked.

"To calm them," Uncle Manfred explained, "the same way a cowboy sings lullabies to his cows. Keeps them from getting spooked and stampeding some direction he doesn't want them to go."

Addie couldn't see any comparison between a raggedy hog driver with a long pole and the exciting, hardy adventures of a cowboy. Why, a hog driver didn't even ride a steed! He just walked the dusty road in old boots. Poor hogs, she thought. They don't have much choice where they're headed.

It wasn't long before Addie and Uncle Manfred passed Sycamore Street and were on their way out of town. The road followed shallow sloughs and lagoons. When they turned west, they crossed a bridge that spanned Beaver Creek, one of many streams that crisscrossed Jackson County and eventually emptied into the wide Mississippi.

The horses' hooves made a hollow *clump! clump! clump!* Addie looked down into the sluggish stream.

"Beaver Creek looks low," Uncle Manfred said, peering over the side of the rickety wooden bridge. "Last time I was farther upstream, I noticed that the old levee's holding pretty well."

"What's a levee?" Addie asked.

"Mounds of dirt on either side of the creek. When the levee holds, it can keep the water from overflowing onto the land."

"Sometimes it doesn't work," Addie said, remembering the big flood three years earlier.

"That's right. Some seasons the river fills all the creeks, and the water seems to have a mind of its own," Uncle Manfred admitted. "Maybe that's why there are so many tall tales about the Mississippi. Just the other day at the station somebody passed along the Oskaloosa newspaper for me to read. And right there on page one I found the report of a seven-foot sea creature that somebody claimed made its way from the Mississippi up the Skunk River—nearly one hundred miles to Oskaloosa."

Addie scooted to safety nearer the middle of the buggy seat and hoped Oskaloosa was very far away. "Was the creature dangerous?"

"The article said the people from the town went after the monster with rifles and revolvers," Uncle Manfred continued. "When bullets failed to penetrate its hide, they shot at it with a cannon loaded with a keg of railroad spikes."

Addie thought she saw her uncle smile. Was he joking? "You can't believe everything you read in the newspapers," she said, using Pa's favorite phrase.

Uncle Manfred laughed. "You're right. Maybe the whole thing's a practical joke. Maybe some newspaper writer made up the monster."

Addie thought of Eleanor and her endless practical jokes. Inviting people to eat sand cakes. Tipping over outhouses. Hiding snakes in sunbonnets. What magnificent, new, wonderful idea did she have for the Fourth of July? To keep from worrying about Eleanor's next reckless scheme, Addie hummed:

> *Hog up! Hog up!*
> *Forty cents a day and no dinner,*
> *straw bed and no cover,*
> *corn bread and no butter.*
> *Hog up! Hog up!*

They started up the dirt road to the farm. After more than a month away, Addie saw her home with new eyes. Paint was peeling from the house. The barn sagged on one end where the big flood had knocked away part of the foundation. Nothing grew in the dusty yard except a scraggly morning glory poking along the fence. Compared to Aunt Ida's and Uncle Manfred's place, everything seemed very shabby.

When they reached the house, Uncle Manfred tied the horses to the porch railing. Nowhere was there any sign of the man who had been hired by Pa to take care of the fields and cattle. "While I look in the barn," Uncle Manfred said, "why don't you go inside and find those baby clothes?"

Addie leapt from the buggy seat. With a noisy thump, she yanked open the front door. How empty and musty-smelling the house was! Even so, she half-expected to hear her brothers' voices or her mother calling everyone for dinner. "Hello? Anybody here?" Addie shouted. She wanted to make sure she gave any hiding outlaws a chance to run out the back way—just in case Eleanor had been right about someone hiding here.

When no one answered, Addie tiptoed upstairs. She peeked into the room she shared with George and Lew and Burt. There was the cat she had drawn in pencil on the wall behind the door. She had made it very small so it would not be noticed. The cat looked so lonesome!

She hurried to the chest of drawers in the hallway. There she found a clean pillowcase to carry the baby clothing back to Mother. She unfolded the tiny shirts one by one. They smelled faintly of sour milk and sweet camphor. She wished they were newer and daintier. Perhaps Mother could add some pink bows here and there.

When she finished packing the shirts, cotton gowns, and flour-sack diapers, Addie went into the kitchen. She spotted a mouse on the shelf over the stove. He scampered away, knocking Pa's pipe onto the floor. Addie picked up the pipe and examined it to make sure it wasn't broken.

Suddenly, she missed her father. She looked around the empty kitchen and could almost see him sitting there at the table, maps spread out before him. Where was he now? Was he thinking of her? She wondered when they would all be together in their own house. A family again.

What if Aunt Ida had been wrong about them staying in Sabula forever? Addie didn't want to think about leaving the town and their farm. She didn't want to think about another girl moving into this house, maybe erasing her secret cat from the wall.

"Hello, my dear!"

Addie jumped.

"Look what I found," Uncle Manfred said. He was carrying the plain wooden cradle that had been used by Addie and all her brothers. "We'll take it back with us. Won't your mother be pleased?"

Addie nodded. But deep down, she didn't want to bring the old cradle to her aunt and uncle's fancy house. It would look so out of place there. "I heard Aunt Ida say she was going to borrow a new spool bed with a canopy," Addie said.

"Family traditions must be maintained," Uncle Manfred insisted. "I happen to know that your great-grandfather built this cradle and brought it when he came from England."

Addie wondered how many babies had already been rocked to sleep in this old cradle. She ran her finger over "GEO," the letters George had carved when nobody was looking. The wood was scarred with other mysterious marks. Who had made them? Other mischievous brothers?

"I talked to the hired man. He was feeding the cows in the barn. Now let's gather some eggs, and we'll be on our way," Uncle Manfred said. He handed her the egg basket.

When Addie had finished in the chicken coop checking the nest of each cantankerous hen for fresh eggs, she climbed into the buggy. As her uncle's horses trotted out of the yard, she turned and gave the weather-beaten farmhouse one last homesick look.

"Goodbye, cat," she whispered.

CHAPTER FIVE

Hollyhock Ladies

"YOU'RE VERY QUIET," Uncle Manfred said as the buggy rolled along. "Anything wrong?"

"Do you think the hired man is taking good care of our farm?" Addie asked.

Uncle Manfred nodded. "Everything seems just fine."

Addie wanted to believe Uncle Manfred. She wanted to believe that everything was just fine. Any day Pa would be home, and her family would move back to the farm and be together again. Life would be just as it was.

She stared along the road ahead. She thought she saw someone waving in the tall weeds off to one side.

"Whoa! Hello there, stranger!" Uncle Manfred called. The buggy rolled to a stop.

Eleanor smiled up at them. In her arms she held a battered bucket filled with raspberries. "Can you give me a ride back to town?"

"Hop up," Addie said. Seeing her friend made her feel more cheerful.

"Where've you been?" Uncle Manfred asked. He clucked his tongue, and the horses started down the road again.

"Picking berries up near Canada Hollow Cemetery," Eleanor said. "Have one." Her sticky red face and hands showed she'd already eaten quite a few.

Addie popped a bright sweet berry into her mouth. "Uncle Manfred, tell Eleanor the story about the Oskaloosa sea monster. Please?"

"I'd be delighted," he said, "as long as you don't get too scared."

"I don't scare easily," Eleanor bragged, and ate another berry. Addie had some, too. By the time Uncle Manfred finished telling the story, they'd reached Pearl Street, and the berry bucket was nearly empty.

"Looks like you girls made a good sampling of those raspberries," Uncle Manfred said. "I bet five dollars there aren't enough in that bucket to make half a pie."

Eleanor groaned. "Ma's going to be furious."

"I've seen raspberries up near Dixon's pasture. We're not too far from there," Addie said. "If we worked together, Eleanor, we could refill that bucket in no time. Would you mind taking the eggs and baby clothes home, Uncle Manfred?"

"I'd be happy to," he said, stopping the buggy. The girls climbed out. "Just be home in time for supper, Addie."

Addie waved goodbye to her uncle. Then she linked arms with Eleanor, and they walked down the road toward Dixon's pasture. It was so unusual not to have her brothers to watch that Addie almost felt as if she were on a holiday.

The girls climbed over a fence. Wind blew through the long grass. Although the Dixons owned the land, they had not lived here in a long time. Wildflowers bloomed along a small stream that crossed one corner of the property. The girls followed the stream, picking raspberries as they went. When the bucket was full, they rested along the bank, where old hollyhocks grew.

Addie held a pale pink hollyhock blossom between her fingers and spun it upside down. "Doesn't this look just like a lady in a ball gown?"

Eleanor nodded and chewed on a piece of grass.

Addie took off her apron, spread it on the ground, and poured the raspberries onto it. Then she filled the bucket with water from the stream.

"What are you doing?" Eleanor asked.

"Watch," Addie said. She floated a hollyhock blossom upside down in the water. When she gently blew on it, the hollyhock lady twirled around and around. "See her dance?"

Eleanor laughed with delight. She picked another blossom and floated it in the bucket. "How do you do?" she said, and made the blossom curtsey. It wasn't long before the bucket had become a crowded ballroom.

"Now it's time for your first swimming lesson," Eleanor announced.

Addie giggled. "I can't shrink as small as a hollyhock lady."

Eleanor plucked out every hollyhock blossom. "George is nowhere in sight. This is your big chance to learn how to hold your breath underwater."

"How?" Addie asked. "There's not enough water in the stream to swim in."

"Just do what I do," Eleanor said. She closed her eyes tight, held her breath, and plunged her face into the bucket. She blew bubbles so fiercely that the water boiled and churned to the rim. "Now you try."

What could be so hard about putting her face in a bucket? She was glad George was not around to make fun of her. Quickly, she lowered her face in and out of the water.

"No," Eleanor said, "it has to be longer than that. And you're supposed to blow bubbles."

Addie took a deep breath and shut her eyes tight. She blew a few bubbles. The water felt cool and refreshing. This was nothing like the way she'd felt when she'd stuck her head into the Mississippi and couldn't see or hear and all the world seemed to have turned upside down. "How was that?" she exclaimed, face dripping.

"Bravo!" Eleanor said. "That's all you have to do. Breathe out, not in, when you're underwater and you won't drown."

"What if I run out of air?"

"Paddle up to the surface, stick your head out of the water, and take a fresh gulp of air," Eleanor said. "Now for the next part of your swimming lesson."

CHAPTER SIX

Swimming Lesson

"WHAT'S THE SECOND PART?" Addie asked nervously.

"Follow me," ordered Eleanor. She tossed the water from the bucket and dumped the raspberries back in. She swung the bucket and walked with such long strides that Addie had trouble keeping up. The girls followed the stream to the place where it emptied into the Mississippi. Here the river current was slow. Coffee-colored water lapped gently at the roots of trees growing along the muddy bank.

Eleanor refused to say one word until they reached a very large tree. She took off her apron and left it carefully folded on the riverbank. She unhooked a long, thick rope that hung from a limb jutting out over the water. Long ago, someone had tied a fat knot at the end.

"Watch me," Eleanor said. She held the rope with both hands, took a running start, and swung out over the water. "Yahooo!" she yelled. At the last moment, Eleanor let go and fell with a loud splash into the river.

She paddled. She blew bubbles. In a few minutes, she had scrambled back up the bank with a watch-out-everybody grin on her face. "Now you try."

Addie took off her shoes. She didn't want to swing out over the water and jump. The rope didn't look safe. Besides, what if she fell off too soon and hit her head on a tree root? She'd forget to blow bubbles. She'd forget not to breathe. And she'd drown for sure. "Couldn't I just wade in slowly and put my head in?"

"Absolutely not," Eleanor said. "Swinging and leaping from the rope is easy and fast. It's one-two-three and you're in the river, swimming. There's no such thing as an Oskaloosa monster. Even your uncle admitted it."

Addie sucked in her breath all at once. Why did Eleanor have to mention the monster? Now she really felt awful.

"Come on. It's easy. Don't be a fraidy cat," Eleanor taunted.

Reluctantly, Addie took the end of the rope. She did not want to be left out of games or be called names anymore. Most of all, she did not want to stand by helplessly while someone nearly drowned. She moved backward a few steps.

"Don't take all day," Eleanor complained. "Are you going to learn to swim or aren't you?"

"What about my clothes? I'll get all wet."

Eleanor rolled her eyes. "Don't worry, your dress will dry fast. It's a hot day."

Addie held the rope. "You'll save me if I go under and forget what to do, right?"

Eleanor nodded. "When I say 'jump,' let go of the rope. You'll be perfectly fine. Trust me."

Addie pulled the rope swing back as far as she could, then ran toward the edge of the embankment. At the last moment, she bravely gripped the rope, lifted her legs, and swung out dizzily over the water.

"Jump!" Eleanor shouted.

The rope swung back to shore. Addie nearly jumped off onto dry land, but somehow her fingers refused to uncurl. Before she knew it, the swing had started out over the river again.

"One-two-three, jump!" Eleanor ordered.

But Addie could not jump. She clung to the rope for dear life.

"Addie!" Eleanor shrieked in disgust. *"Jump!"*

As she swung out over the water a third time, Addie knew she could not let go. Slowly, the swing came to rest. Addie lowered herself to the bank, ashamed.

"How," Eleanor demanded, "do you think you'll ever learn to swim if you don't get wet?"

"Sorry," Addie mumbled. "I felt off balance. I just need some time— "

"Carry the bucket," Eleanor interrupted. She ran her fingers through her tangled, damp hair. "We're going to town."

"What for?" Addie asked.

"I tried to keep up my end of our bargain. I tried

to teach you to swim. Now it's your turn to help me," Eleanor said. She picked up her apron and reached into her pocket. Carefully, she untied a handkerchief containing three coins.

"What's your magnificent, new, wonderful idea?" Addie asked, even though she didn't really want to know. Not now, not after being humiliated again.

"Every Fourth of July, each of my sisters and I get a quarter to spend any way we want," Eleanor said, giving the coins a shake. "I have my quarter, and I convinced my two youngest sisters to give me theirs."

"How did you do that?" Addie asked, impressed by Eleanor's power over her younger sisters.

Eleanor shrugged. She gave Addie the quarters, more money than Addie had ever held in her life.

"What are you going to do with all this?" Addie asked.

"First, we're going to my house to get my doll carriage. Then we're off to Day's Dry Goods," Eleanor said. "We're going to buy something really spectacular for the Fourth of July."

"We are?" Addie said anxiously. "What are we buying?"

"A firecracker," Eleanor whispered. "Not just any firecracker. The biggest, loudest, grandest firecracker ever to wake up Sabula folks on Fourth-of-July morning."

CHAPTER SEVEN

Something Spectacular

ELEANOR PUT HER LARGE RAG DOLL with its one button eye missing into her doll carriage. The girls wheeled the carriage into Day's Dry Goods Store. Eleanor peered up at the shelf of firecrackers behind the crowded counter. Addie pretended to look at a display of waterproof boots.

"Hello, Herbert," Eleanor said to the clerk.

"Hello, Eleanor. How's your sister?"

"You mean Josephine? Bossy as ever," Eleanor said. "She said to say hello if I saw you."

Herbert's thin lips parted so that his rabbitlike teeth showed. Suddenly, he almost looked happy. "Getting ready for the big Independence Day celebration tomorrow? Is your sister going to the picnic at Sugg's Grove?"

"Of course," Eleanor said, and gave Addie an exasperated look.

Herbert sighed.

"Maybe you can help us. We're trying to find something special for the Fourth of July," Eleanor said.

"A little American flag perhaps?" Herbert suggested. "Or what about this?" He held up a red, white, and blue kite. "It's called the Minute Man Flyer."

Eleanor shook her head. "We want a firecracker."

Herbert took down a wooden box filled with strings of penny poppers. "Too babyish," Eleanor said. "We want something loud."

"What about a bunch of five-centers? They make a big bang if you light them all at once," he suggested.

"Not dramatic enough," she said.

"How much money do you have?" Herbert asked.

"Seventy-five cents," Eleanor said.

Herbert arched an eyebrow. "That's still not enough for a Bengal Light or a Roman Pinwheel."

Eleanor groaned with disappointment.

"Wait right here," Herbert said. "Maybe I can find something in the storeroom."

He returned in a few minutes, holding something big and fat wrapped in frilly red paper. "I bet you'll like this. It's a Deluxe George Washington Patriot Sky Rocket."

"Will it make a big noise?" Eleanor asked.

"Enough to wake the dead."

Addie gasped. She did not like the idea of waking up dead people.

"This beauty costs a lot more than seventy-five cents," Herbert whispered, "but I'm giving it to you at a special bargain rate."

"Say, that's really generous of you, Herbert," Eleanor said.

Addie handed him the money. Eleanor slipped the Deluxe George Washington Patriot Sky Rocket under the blanket in the carriage.

"You be careful with this firecracker. It's pretty powerful," Herbert said, and coughed nervously. "And you'll say hello to Josephine for me, won't you, Eleanor?"

"Sure, sure," Eleanor replied. "I'll tell her anything you like. Only promise you'll keep this firecracker a secret. Can you do that, Herbert?"

Herbert nodded eagerly. "Tell Josephine...tell her..." He blushed.

"Tell her what?" Eleanor said impatiently.

"Tell her I'll meet her at Sugg's Grove tomorrow at noon," he mumbled quickly.

"Sugg's Grove tomorrow at noon," Eleanor said. She waved and hurried out the door.

Addie followed, pushing the doll carriage. "That fellow sure acted funny," she said. "Like he just ate too many green apples or something."

"He's sweet on my sister. Can't see why," Eleanor said. "Josephine doesn't have the slightest idea how to enjoy the Fourth of July. But we do, don't we? This will be the best Fourth of July ever!"

Addie didn't have a chance to answer. Eleanor was moving too fast down the boardwalk with the doll carriage, trying to avoid the bumps. Suddenly, Addie stopped. "Eleanor," she asked, "where are you going to set off the firecracker?"

Eleanor smiled. "My father says firecrackers cannot be set off near the house. But there's one place he never mentioned."

"Where's that?"

Eleanor whispered something in her ear. "You have to keep a secret," Eleanor said. "Nobody said I couldn't do it, so I'm not breaking the rules. Besides, it's a grand way to start the Fourth of July, don't you think?"

Addie didn't answer. She felt too sick to her stomach. When they reached Aunt Ida's house, Eleanor grabbed her arm. "You take the doll carriage inside and hide the firecracker somewhere. There are plenty of empty rooms in that big house."

"What?" Addie said, stunned.

"I can't take the firecracker home," Eleanor hissed. "One of my nosey sisters will be sure to find it." She put her hands on her hips. "You said you'd help me. You better not go back on your word."

Addie couldn't think of what to say. A firecracker in Aunt Ida's house? What if it exploded by accident? "Wh-where am I supposed to keep it?" she stammered.

"Somewhere safe, of course," Eleanor said. "A deal's a deal. I tried to teach you to swim. Now it's your turn to help me. You only have to hide it a little while. I'll be back for it tonight."

Before Addie could refuse, Eleanor had scampered down the street.

CHAPTER EIGHT

Bad News

ADDIE WHEELED THE BABY BUGGY inside the front hall. Where was she going to hide a firecracker? She heard a noise upstairs. She had to hurry. She glanced inside the empty parlor—Aunt Ida's praying chair! Addie scooped up the firecracker, still wrapped in the doll blanket, and slid it under the frilly ruffle at the bottom of the chair.

"Hello, Addie," said Aunt Ida.

Addie leapt up. "Hello," she said, her heart beating fast.

"I thought I heard you. Did you lose something?"

"No," Addie said. "I was just taking this doll for a stroll around the parlor." She glanced at the rag doll, which had been flung upside down in the carriage. Quickly she turned it right side up. Why did it seem as if its one button eye was laughing at her?

"I've been thinking we should plan s   pleasant amusement," Aunt Ida said. "You seem so sad and blue these days. I know, how about a tea party for your doll?"

Addie nodded. "But the doll isn't mine. It's Eleanor's. She lent it to me."

"That's even better. A guest of honor," Aunt Ida said. She hurried into the kitchen to prepare one of her famous graham cracker and lemonade teas, served on a miniature real china tea set from France.

On the porch table she spread Addie's favorite table-cloth, the one with the yellow daisies on it.

"Come sit down, ladies," Aunt Ida said to Addie and the doll. Aunt Ida set out the cups and saucers.

Usually, Addie loved to have a tea party with Aunt Ida. But today she could not enjoy herself. She couldn't stop thinking about the Deluxe George Washington Patriot Sky Rocket that might explode in the parlor any minute.

After supper, as soon as the fireflies began to dart in and out of Uncle Manfred's rosebushes, Eleanor appeared at the back door.

"Hello, Eleanor. Go right in. Addie's inside," Aunt Ida said. She sat on the porch with Mother and Uncle Manfred. George, Lew, and Burt were practicing cartwheels in the backyard.

Addie pulled Eleanor into the empty parlor. "I'm not supposed to be in here," she whispered. "We'll have to be quick about it."

"What are you two doing?" George said, ducking his head in the doorway. "You're not allowed in there, you know."

"We're just admiring Aunt Ida's china dogs. Now leave us alone," Addie said in a low voice.

"You better not break anything," George said. He went outside. Through the parlor window, Addie could see him jumping leapfrog over the cistern, the barrel-like tank built to catch rainwater. While he jumped, Addie and Eleanor whisked up the firecracker and slipped it into Eleanor's doll carriage.

By the time the girls came outside, George had pried open the lid of the cistern and was making echoing noises by shouting into it at the top of his lungs.

"What are you doing?" Addie demanded.

"There's hardly enough rainwater for me to drown down there, if that's what you're worried about," George said with a smirk.

Addie would have liked to smack her brother, but she didn't.

"Shut the cistern, George," she said in an even voice. "You're going to give Lew bad ideas if he sees what you're doing."

"You're no fun," George complained. "I'm going to go catch fireflies and pull off their lights."

Addie watched her brother disappear around the bushes into the backyard.

"I have one more favor to ask," Eleanor said.

Addie sighed.

"Sneak out of bed early tomorrow and come to my house. Help me with the grand surprise," Eleanor said eagerly. "You won't want to miss it."

Addie thought for a moment. What if the Deluxe George Washington Patriot Sky Rocket really did wake the dead?

"Are you going to come or not?"

Addie hesitated. If she said yes, she might get into

terrible trouble. "I can't," she said at last. "Sorry."

"You're such a fraidy cat," Eleanor said angrily. "You won't swim. You won't help me when I do something important. Well, I guess you're not my friend anymore. I never want to speak to you again, Addie Mills."

She turned and marched away, pushing her doll carriage with the Deluxe George Washington Patriot Sky Rocket tucked inside it.

Sadly, Addie watched her best friend disappear down the street. She shuffled up the porch steps.

"What's wrong, child?" Aunt Ida asked.

Addie only shrugged her shoulders. She spent the rest of the evening watching Burt and Lew so that Aunt Ida and Mother could finish baking pies for the Fourth-of-July picnic the next day.

"Tell me a story!" Lew begged.

But Addie couldn't think of anything that wasn't very, very sad. Burt fell asleep on a blanket under the dining room table. Lew pushed a wooden horse around and around in circles, while Addie lay on her back and looked up at the ceiling. Everything seemed so boring without Eleanor. What would life be like if they never spoke again?

Finally, Lew dozed off, too, his sticky cheek resting against his outstretched arm. Addie was about to go and tell Mother that Lew and Burt were ready to be carried up to bed, when she heard worried voices coming from the kitchen.

"…after the flood in '80," Mother said, "we never got back on our feet. We still owe rent. And with the dry spring this year, I'm not sure there's going to be a crop worth harvesting. I can't help worrying what's going to happen to us this winter."

"If it's another loan you need," Aunt Ida said, "I'm certain Manfred would be willing to help."

"You've been more than generous. But I don't know when we'll repay your first kindness," Mother replied. "Samuel is so determined to start over in Dakota. He can file on 160 acres there, and the land will be ours. We've never owned our own land."

Addie held her breath. *Start over in Dakota.* What did Mother mean?

"Men are silly creatures," Aunt Ida continued. "They get these ideas in their heads to drag their families out where there's nothing but grass and sky. What kind of place is that to raise a family? No, when Samuel returns, he'll realize what he has here in Sabula. He won't tear up all his roots and move. I'm sure you'll do fine next year and if you don't, we can always help you."

"Samuel is very proud. He appreciates everything you've done, but I know he won't ask for another loan. He's stubborn. He told me before he left that if he found just the right piece of land, we'd leave for Dakota as soon as this baby's born."

Leave as soon as this baby is born? Addie leaned

forward to hear more and accidentally set the dining room door swinging.

"Who's there?" Aunt Ida called.

Addie stumbled through the doorway. She wanted to shout, "No, we can't leave!" But instead she said, "Lew's asleep."

"My goodness," Aunt Ida said, looking at the kitchen clock. "It's past your bedtime, Addie. Go on upstairs. Uncle Manfred and I will carry Lew and Burt up."

"I'm not going," Addie said, suddenly bursting with anger. Her aunt was the one who'd assured her they were staying in Sabula where they belonged. "Aunt Ida, why did you lie to me?"

Mother gasped. "Addie! What are you saying? Apologize to your aunt at once."

Aunt Ida raised her hand as if to silence Mother. "What did I lie about?"

"About leaving. You said we weren't going to

Dakota. And now we are. You knew all along," Addie said, her fists clenched. "It isn't fair."

"Addie, you cannot blame Aunt Ida for not knowing," Mother said. "I only told her just now."

Addie didn't say anything for several moments. "I'm sorry, Aunt Ida," she mumbled finally, even though she didn't mean it. She wasn't sorry. Not a bit.

"And I'm sorry, too," Aunt Ida replied, dabbing her eyes with her handkerchief. "I can't bear the thought of you moving."

"Nothing's for certain yet," Mother said softly. "I was waiting to talk to you, Addie, as soon as your father returned."

Nothing's for certain. Addie knew what that meant. It meant they were moving, and she had no choice but to accept the awful fact. She stomped up the steps, went into her bedroom, and slammed the door.

She threw herself on the bed and sobbed. In one day, she had lost her best friend and found out that her family was leaving Sabula for good. Addie blew her nose as hard as she could. As for the new baby, she didn't want it anymore. Even if it was a girl.

CHAPTER NINE

Runaway!

BOOM! BOOM! BOOM! Addie opened one eye. What was that sound? Why, fireworks, of course. It was morning, and today was the Fourth of July.

For one brief moment, Addie felt happy. Then she recalled what had happened the night before.

She remembered Eleanor's angry words and the scene in the kitchen with Aunt Ida and Mother.

"We're moving," she told herself. She wouldn't get to go to school in the fall, to the new brick schoolhouse that had just been built. She wouldn't be able to pick raspberries with Eleanor or play with her cousins. There'd be no more visits to Grandpa's house, no more tea parties with Aunt Ida, no more stories told by Uncle Manfred.

Even worse than thinking about leaving was imagining the wide open, lonely place they'd soon be going to. Dakota. How would they survive where there was nothing but grass and sky?

Miserably, she rolled over, a pillow pressed against her ears. She did not care anymore about the Fourth of July. She'd stay in bed all day.

Boom! Boom! Boom!

"Addie!" George shouted, pounding on the bedroom door. "Open up. Uncle Manfred wants to talk to you right this minute, and you'd better hurry because he's not joking."

Addie leapt out of bed, still dressed from the night before. Through the window she could see a grey sky. Rain pelted against the glass. She opened the door. There stood George in his straw cowboy hat, which he'd decorated with a red, white, and blue ribbon. His carved wooden six-shooters stuck out of his pockets. "You're in trouble," he said, grinning.

Addie went slowly downstairs. Her aunt was probably still mad at her about her rude comments the night before. She sighed, wishing she could disappear.

"Addie?" called Aunt Ida. "Please come in here, child."

Steam coated the windows of the kitchen. Pots boiled on the stove. The table was covered with picnic hampers, jars of relish and watermelon pickles, loaves of bread, and all kinds of cake. "Your uncle has something important to ask you," Aunt Ida said, her hair hanging in limp ringlets around her face.

"If it's about last night, I'm sorry for what I said. Really I am," Addie said softly so that George couldn't hear.

"I know. You were upset. Happens to all of us," Aunt Ida said, and gave Addie a hug. "This is something else, something to do with your friend."

"Eleanor?" Addie asked. Her stomach lurched. What had happened?

"Go talk to your uncle. He's in the dining room trying to pin on his parade sash," Aunt Ida said.

Addie tiptoed into the dining room. Uncle Manfred stood near the table, awkwardly struggling to attach a red, white, and blue sash around his shoulder. "Why does everything have to happen on the one morning it shouldn't?" he said to no one in particular. "At the station we just received a tele-

96

graph that the levee's out. It's been raining all night, and the river's rising. You'd think the Mississippi would cooperate once in a blue moon. But no. It's the Fourth of July, and all blasted havoc breaks loose."

"Manfred!" Aunt Ida scolded from the kitchen. "Not in front of the children!"

"There!" Uncle Manfred said, finally fastening the sash.

"What is it you wanted to ask me?" Addie said in a small voice. She could sense George behind her, sneaky and silent as a shadow.

"Ah, yes," Uncle Manfred said. "While I was up early on my way back from the station, I saw all kinds of commotion going on in the Fitzgeralds' yard. It appeared that they'd had some kind of explosion. Rocked the entire neighborhood."

"Explosion!" George said. "I wish I could have been there to see it."

Uncle Manfred shook his head. "George, I don't think this is the kind of explosion anyone would want to witness too closely."

The Deluxe George Washington Patriot Sky Rocket! "Was...was anyone hurt?" Addie whispered.

"No, fortunately," Uncle Manfred said. "It seems some vicious scoundrel lowered an enormous firecracker down the Fitzgeralds' cistern. When the firecracker blew up, the cistern cover flew sky high. When the cover came down, it beheaded most of Mr. Fitzgerald's prize roses."

"Oh," said Addie. What would Uncle Manfred do when he found out that she'd helped buy and hide that enormous firecracker?

"Do you have any idea," Uncle Manfred continued, "where Eleanor might be? She's missing."

"Missing?" Addie asked.

"Her family's frantic. After the commotion died

down a little, her folks began to check to make sure everyone in the family was all right. That's when her mother found Eleanor's bed was empty, and her father realized their horse was gone. No one's sure, but they think that she may have had something to do with the firecracker prank."

"She's run away!" George yodeled. He twirled his six-shooters on his fingers. "Just like a runaway out-law!"

"That's quite enough, George," Uncle Manfred scolded sternly. "No one knows where she's gone. But she may be in terrible danger. The levee's given way, and we can't be sure how high the water's going to rise. A search party's already combing the banks of the river."

Addie took a deep breath. "I saw Eleanor last night," she admitted. "She was angry at me when she left. I haven't seen her since." Somehow Addie could not make herself tell her uncle anything more.

"Keep an eye out for her, will you, Addie and George?" Uncle Manfred said. "I must go down to Sugg's Grove and assist with preparations. I'll be going to join the search party later."

Addie watched her uncle leave. "That poor, poor girl! Her family must be worried sick," Aunt Ida exclaimed. "Children, I want you to promise me you won't wander away. The river's running wild. Now don't you worry, Addie. I'm sure Eleanor will be found safe and sound. In the meantime, we have much to get ready. Your mother's going to need all your help, Addie. Addie—are you listening?"

Addie nodded, but she had not heard a word her aunt said. Where was Eleanor? Was she hurt? She *had* to go and find her.

As soon as Mother and Aunt Ida had gone back into the kitchen, Addie grabbed her cloak and slipped out the front door. She didn't even stop to think.

She hurried down Pearl Street, making her way around puddles, past the wagons coming into town, filled with families and picnic baskets.

The rain came down harder. She paused to draw her cloak around her shoulders. She knew Eleanor was in terrible trouble. That's why she'd run away. Addie shivered as she turned George's words over in her mind. *Just like a runaway outlaw.*

In that instant, she knew where Eleanor had gone. She was in the one place no one would ever look. Eleanor was hiding in the Mills's empty farmhouse!

Addie dashed out from under the tree. She leapt over puddles and dodged wagons on her way out of town. She made good time until she came to Beaver Creek. Even before she reached the bridge, she knew something was very wrong. A low, unfamiliar roar filled the air, making her think of the Oskaloosa monster. What was it?

She looked upstream. The bridge was gone—washed away. The once clear, sleepy creek was deep brown, churning wider and deeper than she'd ever seen it, pushing up over the embankment. There had been no way to get to the farmhouse without going across the bridge.

What if Eleanor had tried to swim across and was caught by the current, just like that child Aunt Ida had talked about?

Swept away. The very idea of being dragged under, sucked breathless, blind, and dizzy, was so awful that Addie considered turning back. She'd go home and get help. Somebody older, stronger. Somebody who knew how to swim.

She took a few steps back toward the road, then paused. At that moment, she could see little Lew in the water again, flailing, shouting as they'd come around the bend. He had nearly drowned in that one brief instant! How quickly it had happened!

Tree branches floated past. Then a fence post, a wooden crate, a chair, a dead chicken. And the next time she looked down, raging water had inched up nearly to where she stood.

What if she were too late? What if Eleanor had already gone under, trying to ford the river? No, Addie decided. She had to keep searching. She had to find her friend. "Eleanor!" she screamed. "Where are you?"

The only answer was the rush of Beaver Creek. There was another bridge downriver, but Addie didn't know how far it was. Still, there was nothing else to do but try to get to that other bridge. Maybe Eleanor was ahead of her, trying to do the same thing.

Addie walked on and on along the creek bank. She picked her way over tree roots and fallen branches. Rain soaked through her cloak. Mud caked her shoes. She called for Eleanor, always keeping her eye on the rushing water, searching for some sign. When she was about to give up, she saw something flash beyond a bush. It looked like a scarf whipped in the wind or the curling tail of a river monster.

Addie crept closer. A whinny filled the air. The monster was no monster. It was Vulcan!

He was tied to a tree, swishing his tail and stomping. When the big horse saw her, he backed up as far as his frayed rope would allow.

"There, there," Addie said softly, patting his neck. She was so happy to find the horse. Eleanor *must* be nearby. "Vulcan, where is she?" Addie whispered. She stared intently over the water and saw something that made her shudder. Eleanor—clinging to a fallen tree.

"Eleanor!" Addie shouted.

"Help!" Eleanor screamed. "Throw me something and pull me in!"

Addie knew she had to move fast. "I'm coming," she called, even though she had no idea how she'd reach her friend. The swollen creek was creeping higher. Soon the water would cover Eleanor's perch.

Desperately, she searched for a branch, but there was nothing the right length or strength. Vulcan's rope was not long enough to throw to Eleanor, but seeing the old horse standing patiently in the rain gave Addie an idea.

"I'll come out to you on Vulcan," she shouted. "Call to him. When we get close enough, jump on his back."

"Hurry!" Eleanor cried.

Addie untied Vulcan. She spoke gently to him as she struggled to climb on his back. Vulcan balked, but somehow she managed to turn his head toward the river. She kicked his wide flanks with her muddy heels.

"Vulcan!" Eleanor said. "Come on, boy."

Vulcan refused to go into the raging creek.

More branches and part of a fence sped past. Addie gripped the horse's mane so tightly that her knuckles went white. If only she could swim! Then, perhaps, she wouldn't feel so afraid. "He won't budge," she called to Eleanor.

"He has to! Make him!" Eleanor shouted.

Addie kicked hard. Vulcan took a few stumbling steps down the embankment and into the water. One false step and he'd fall, roll over, and dump her into the creek. The end. A horrible watery end. She looked up and saw Eleanor's pleading face. She could not give up.

She kicked Vulcan again, and he took another step. Now her feet hung in the water. To keep him calm and give him courage, she sang in his ear the first song that came to her:

Hog up! Hog up!
Forty cents a day and no dinner,
straw bed and no cover,
corn bread and no butter.
Hog up! Hog up!

Slowly, Vulcan lowered himself into the water and made his way toward Eleanor. "Come on! You can do it!" Eleanor called to him encouragingly. She reached out to Addie. Addie grabbed with one hand, but she couldn't reach her friend. They were still too far apart.

"Closer!" Eleanor cried. "This branch won't hold much longer."

"Come on, Vulcan," Addie said in his ear. The horse took another lurching step. Gripping his mane with all her strength, she barely avoided plunging over his head into the water. Somehow she regained her balance and again extended her arm. This time she grabbed Eleanor's sleeve, then held tight to her arm at the elbow.

"Don't let go," Eleanor begged. Using Addie's arm as an anchor, she pulled herself onto Vulcan. The horse stumbled as Eleanor flopped across his back.

"Turn him around," Eleanor ordered. "Head to shore."

Addie pulled at his halter. She kicked. Vulcan did not need any encouragement. He lifted his hooves and splashed toward dry land, up the embankment, three, four steps...safe at last!

CHAPTER TEN

Forever Friends

As the girls looked back, Eleanor's branch heaved upward and was sucked under the rushing water. Addie's teeth chattered so hard she could barely speak. "What were you doing out there?" she demanded.

"I heard barking," Eleanor said, sliding down

from the horse. "A yellow dog was caught in the current, and he tried to climb on that pile of branches. Before I could reach him, he disappeared."

She looked up at Addie and burst into tears. "I was so scared out there. I wouldn't have had a chance if you hadn't come along." She buried her face in Vulcan's neck.

Addie felt stunned. She had never considered that Eleanor might be afraid of anything. She slipped off Vulcan and hugged Eleanor, who sobbed and sobbed as if her heart would break.

"I'm sorry I called you fraidy cat," Eleanor said, wiping her eyes. "You were amazingly brave to go out there. I bet now you could learn to swim."

Addie smiled. She *had* been brave. Learning to swim couldn't be as hard as what she'd just been through, could it? "I promise I'll be a faster learner," she said, glad to have their friendship mended. "We don't have much time."

Eleanor looked at her with confused, red eyes. "What do you mean?"

Addie's smile vanished. "We're moving to Dakota as soon as this baby is born," she said. "Mother told me yesterday."

For once, Eleanor seemed unable to think of anything to say.

"You can write to me," Addie said slowly.

Eleanor blinked. "They have post offices out there?"

"Sure," Addie replied, trying her best to sound bright and cheerful.

"I'm not as good at writing as you," Eleanor replied. "Who'll help me with reading when you're gone away? Who'll make up hollyhock ladies and hide my firecrackers?" Without warning, she was sobbing again.

"You can send a telegram," Addie said, patting her shoulder. "Uncle Manfred will let you send it from the station. Maybe he'll let you twirl in his office chair."

"He will?" Eleanor said, sniffing loudly. "All the same, I'd rather have you here than gone away to Dakota."

"Me, too," Addie said. "I don't really want to go." Vulcan impatiently stomped his front hoof. Addie rubbed the horse's nose and blinked back tears.

"You won't ever forget me, will you, Addie?" Eleanor asked.

"Never," Addie said. "We're forever friends." She smiled, thinking of what Aunt Ida had told her. A sister was a forever friend. So was someone like Eleanor. "We'd better get home. Everyone's worried to death about you."

By the time they reached town, the rain had stopped. On the steps of the First Methodist Church, small boys in tall boots splashed each other. Addie and Eleanor sloshed up to their knees and then up to their waists in water. The horse struggled.

Someone called to them. Uncle Manfred!

Addie laughed when she saw him rowing up Pearl Street. He was still wearing his red, white, and blue sash. Everything was topsy-turvy on this Fourth of July.

"Hello," he shouted. "Are you girls all right? We've been looking everywhere for you."

The girls climbed into the rowboat and told Uncle Manfred what had happened. Uncle Manfred tied Vulcan to the stern. He rowed Eleanor to her house, where her family rushed out, her sisters talking and crying all at once. Sheepishly, Eleanor went inside.

Eleanor's father led brave Vulcan to dry ground. "Thank you for bringing her back to us!" Mr. Fitzgerald called to Uncle Manfred.

"Don't thank me. It was Addie who saved Eleanor," Uncle Manfred said proudly. Then he turned the boat up Pearl Street again, and together he and Addie headed for home.

"Thank the Lord you're safe!" Aunt Ida cried from the porch. Mother and the boys hurried out.

"Addie, you look wet as a drowned rat," George said, and grinned.

For once, Addie didn't mind his teasing.

The Fourth-of-July picnic was small and soggy. Only a few people gathered under umbrellas at Sugg's Grove. There was no parade because the street was underwater. To cheer the picnickers, the Sabula Brass-and-Cornet Concert Band played a few tunes while huddled beneath two trees.

Slowly, the floodwater went down. Carpeting and curtains were hung out to dry. River mud was scrubbed from floors and walls. Little by little, life in Sabula returned to the way it had been before the flood.

As the summer went on, the only signs of the terrible storm were washed-out bridges, toppled fences, and high-water marks on trees and telegraph poles.

As often as they could during the next several weeks, Addie and Eleanor hurried to a quiet bend in the river. Addie didn't want to alarm Aunt Ida or Mother by telling them where they were going. But most of all, she didn't want George or Lew to find out. "My swimming lessons are secret," she told Eleanor. "I don't want anyone to know."

On this particular August morning, the sun shone brightly and the water felt almost warm. "Addie, today's the big day," Eleanor called from the bank. "Put your whole head in this time. Stick your hands out in front and kick to shore the way I showed you."

Addie stood waist deep in the river, six feet from the river's edge. Her bare feet were beginning to sink into the soft mud.

She knew it was now or never. *Swim!* she told herself. The shore wasn't that far, was it? Not any farther than she had gone on Vulcan's back to rescue Eleanor.

Addie closed her eyes tight, took a deep breath, and plunged forward, kicking with all her might. *Whoosh!* She blew underwater bubbles. Her arms paddled. Her legs thrashed.

No more air. She kept moving, even though her chest ached. At last, gravel brushed her fingers. She staggered to her feet, dripping and smiling. She'd made it to shore!

"Hurrah!" Eleanor cheered. "You were swimming! You were really swimming!"

"Yes!" Addie shouted joyfully. She gave Eleanor a playful splash. "I can swim!"

Suddenly, a familiar voice spoiled everything. "Addie!" George called from behind a bush. "You'd better get home right away. Aunt Ida's been looking everywhere for you." He took off like a streak through the woods, back toward town.

Addie scrambled up the river bank, slipped on her shoes, and grabbed her apron. "Bet I'm in big trouble," she said, brushing the dripping strands of hair from her face. "But thanks for helping me."

Eleanor grinned.

Addie ran home. What was wrong? Why were George and Lew waving to her so wildly from the front porch steps? "Hurry up, slowpoke!" George shouted.

Lew tugged her muddy hand and jumped up and down. "Come on!"

"You'll never guess!" George said, beaming. "While you were gone—"

"Hush," Uncle Manfred said from the front doorway. "Don't ruin the surprise!"

Addie felt confused, soggy, and bedraggled. What had happened? She walked in the door and followed

Uncle Manfred up the steps to the second floor.

Aunt Ida stood in the hallway smiling. But when she embraced Addie, her face filled with concern. "You're soaking wet, child. Don't you know you'll catch your death of cold? Where have you been?"

"The river," Addie said. "Eleanor's been teaching me. I can do it, Aunt Ida! I can swim!"

Before she could tell Aunt Ida anything more, George and Lew pulled her toward the bedroom.

There in the big bed, under Aunt Ida's best coverlet, was Mother, looking very small. And beside her was something even smaller—a new baby.

Mother drew Addie closer. She pulled her down and kissed her cheek. Addie stared at the bright pink sleeping face of the baby.

Mother smiled. "Nellie May is several weeks early."

Nellie May! Her own little sister. Her forever friend.

Mother unfolded the soft blanket and showed Addie an impossibly small hand curled like a new fern frond. Addie stroked the little dimples on each knuckle.

The baby's eyelids fluttered open. Nellie May looked directly at Addie with filmy blue eyes and gripped her finger tightly.

Addie smiled, speechless. Nellie May was clearly too small to do chores or play tea party. Even so, Addie could hardly wait to tell Eleanor. Her own sister—at last!

Then she thought of something else, something sad. "Does this mean," she asked Mother, "we'll be going soon? You said, as soon as the baby comes—"

"Dear heart, not right away. Not until the baby gets a little bigger and stronger. And Pa returns."

Addie sighed. "He would have liked to have been here, wouldn't he?"

Mother smiled and nodded.

Burt cried from his bed in the other room. Aunt Ida hurried to pick him up. Suddenly, George and Lew marched into the bedroom. They had tried to be very helpful by stuffing the cradle with every favorite soft blanket until there was hardly room for a baby at all.

"That's very kind of you," Aunt Ida said as she came in with Burt.

"George," Uncle Manfred asked, with a playful gleam in his eye, "does this mean you're not going to float your new baby sister down the river?"

"Yes," George said gruffly, "I guess we'll keep her. She'll be handy for Addie when we get to Dakota. Somebody just for her."

Addie chuckled softly, pleased that George knew about their trip, too.

"I can hardly wait to go to Dakota," George said. "I'm going to eat in a tent, live on a steed, and sleep under the stars without a blanket or fire."

The hardy, adventurous life. What would happen to them in Dakota? Addie wondered. One thing was for certain. They'd all be together again, in their own house. And this time, they'd be on their own land. That was all that mattered, wasn't it? Pa and Mother, George, Lew, and Burt, and Nellie May, too. Everything would turn out all right.

She turned to Mother. "Can I hold her, please?" she asked.

"Of course," Mother said softly.

"But Becca, Addie's quite damp and filthy from swimming in the river," Aunt Ida protested. "Just look at her."

"Eleanor taught me," Addie said. "I kicked all the way to shore with my head underwater."

"Good for you," Mother said, smiling. Then she turned to Aunt Ida. "Let Addie hold the baby. Mississippi mud never hurt anyone."

"Don't just stand there, Manfred! Get the special

chair!" Aunt Ida ordered. "The most comfortable chair for rocking babies. You know which one I mean."

Obediently, Uncle Manfred hurried downstairs to the parlor. Huffing and puffing, he carried the praying chair into the bedroom. Addie sat in the chair. Aunt Ida set Burt on the bed. Then she lifted Nellie May and placed her in her big sister's arms.

Holding the baby carefully, Addie closed her eyes and rocking, rocking, rocking, said something so very quiet that only Nellie May could hear.

Author's Note

Addie's Forever Friend and the four other books about the Mills family (*Addie Across the Prairie*, *Addie's Dakota Winter*, *Addie's Long Summer*, and *George on His Own*) are based on the experiences of my great-grandparents and their children in the 1880s in Iowa and the Dakota Territory. To write these books, I did extensive detective work—tracking down old letters, diaries, and reminiscences as well as newspapers and photographs.

On one expedition to Sabula, Iowa, I brought along an ancient family photo, hoping to use it to find my great-aunt's ornate Victorian house. Years ago, this had been the location of numerous family reunions.

My search seemed fruitless, and just when I was about to give up, a group of local children came to my rescue. They looked at the photo, and one child said, "See that fancy cement cistern cover? We walk past it every day on the way to school." Then they showed me the spot!

Sure enough, the cistern cover was located on what would have been my great-aunt's property. Although the house was gone, I felt grateful to have found at least one old family relic—the cistern cover, which over the years had been used for countless games of tag and leapfrog.

—*Laurie Lawlor*